Maya

and the Stage Fright

Vicky Weber

Written by Vicky Weber

Illustrated by Aleksander Jasinski

To Joey:
Never doubt your talent. Never give up on what you love.

To Christian and Sebastian:
Dream big dreams and then make them happen.
You both inspire me.

Maya loved to sing. She sang in the shower. She sang while she walked to school. Sometimes, she would sing herself to sleep. But most of all, Maya loved to sing with her choir.

They sang fast songs, slow songs, happy songs, sad songs, and everything in between. The choir teacher, Miss Odele, loved all her students and made singing fun.

"Good news, everyone! Our very first concert is next week. Don't forget to invite your friends and family," Miss Odele announced one day.

The week flew by and before Maya knew it, the day of the concert arrived. She was very excited to show her family what they had been working so hard on.

8

The choir lined up behind the stage curtain. Maya poked her head out to see if she could catch a glimpse of her parents in the crowd. She froze. Every single seat was filled. There were even people standing at the back! They had cameras and phones all aimed at the stage to capture their performance. A sinking feeling hit Maya suddenly. Her hands started to sweat, and the color drained from her face.

9

"What's wrong, Maya?" her friend Adriel asked.

She wanted to scream, but when she opened her mouth, no sound came out. She wasn't sure which was worse, the idea of singing in front of all of those people, or the awful feeling in her gut.

Adriel ran off and returned with Miss Odele in tow.

The teacher bent down to Maya's level. "What's going on?" she asked with a soft smile.

"I... don't know," Maya managed to croak, "I peeked out at the crowd..."

"Ah," Miss Odele said, "that sounds like a case of stage fright."

"What's that?" she asked, wiping away a tear.

"Stage fright is when your body reacts to you being nervous. In this case, nervous about singing in front of all those people on stage."
"But I love to sing! How do I make it stop?"

Miss Odele looked left and right. "Can I tell you a secret?"

Maya nodded.

"I still get nervous on stage too."

Maya was shocked. "Really? But you're the music teacher!"

Miss Odele smiled at her. "Oh, yes. Even the best musicians get a case of stage fright! That feeling doesn't always go away but there are things you can do to help."

"You can take slow,
deep breaths, like this."

16

Now, you give it a try!

"Or you can shift your mindset. Instead of thinking about what can go wrong, think about what can go right. What's the best thing that could happen?"

Maya smiled. "My parents could hear me sing. I know they'd be proud of all my hard work!"

Now, you give it a try!

"I have thought of another one, Miss Odele," Maya said.
"I can remind myself that I CAN DO THIS!"

¡Sí se puede!

"You're right, Maya. I know you can do this! Just remember, you might still feel nervous and that's okay, but you don't have to let it stop you from doing something you love."

22

Thanks, Miss Odele. I think I'm ready to go on stage now.

"That's the spirit!" Miss Odele beamed.

"Places, everyone!"

The choir found their places on the risers. Maya was front and center. She felt the stage fright start to take over again, but…

She took some deep breaths.
She thought about the best that could happen.
And she told herself: I can do this!

The piano accompaniment began
and the choir started to sing,
but none as radiantly as Maya.

More musical books by Vicky Weber

Help the tiger win the race.
Tap the beat to keep his pace.

What could be more magical than being a part of the story? Join Tiger in this educational, interactive picture book that focuses on musical vocabulary...and fun!

Abuela made cookies to eat after school.
The gingersnap kind, just the thought made us drool!
We rushed home excited. We opened the door...

...The cookies were missing—just crumbs on the floor!

Can you help the kids crack the case of the Gingersnap Snatcher?

www.trunkupbooks.com

More musical books by Vicky Weber

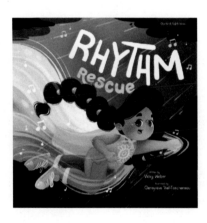

Welcome to Music Metropolis, where there's always a song to sing and instruments playing all around. Everyone has something special to share, but Beat Street is where the real magic happens ...

Step loves stepping up and down the musical staff, but his world is turned upside down when he meets Skip: an adventurous character who isn't afraid of a little risk. Together, they discover that the best music has a little of Step AND Skip!

www.trunkupbooks.com

More musical books by Vicky Weber

Every year, Calla and her family participate in the town's showcase, but this year, she is determined to create a song garden without the help of her parents. Her friends all have great ideas, but writing a song doesn't come as easily to Calla. There are so many choices...what if she gets it wrong?

Lazlo Lemur is nervous about his first day at a new school, especially when he goes to music class. His teacher expects him to learn a new instrument, but there are so many things to remember...

...will he EVER get it right?

www.trunkupbooks.com

About the Author

Vicky Weber is a musician and an elementary educator with a love for children's literature. As a Puerto Rican author of Taíno descent, she strives to create picture books that are fun, engaging, and educational. All her current titles are based on her background in music education or her heritage.

While she has taught a variety of grade levels, primary level education is where her passion lies. It has long been a dream of hers to teach children through the magic of books and she hopes you love reading her works as much as she loved writing them.